For Clara

First U.S. edition 2009

Library of Congress Cataloging-in-Publication Data is available.

Library of Congress Catalog Card Number 2009018405

ISBN 978-0-7636-4411-6

10 9 8 7 6 5 4 3 2 1

Printed in China

This book was typeset in Cochin.
The illustrations were done in mixed media.

Candlewick Press
99 Dover Street
Somerville, Massachusetts 02144

visit us at www.candlewick.com

THE DOLLHOUSE FAIRY

Jane Ray

CANDLEWICK PRESS

ROSY LOVED HER DOLLHOUSE.

It was her favorite thing in the whole world because her dad had built it just for her. Rosy and Dad made the furniture together and collected all sorts of things to put in the different rooms. She played for hours, making up games and stories for the dolls that lived there.

The little house was perfect.

On Saturday mornings, Dad and
Rosy always got up early.
"Just me and my Rosy Posy,"
Dad sang as he made hot chocolate
and French toast for breakfast.

Then Rosy and Dad would make special things for the dollhouse. It was Rosy's favorite time.

But one windy Saturday, when Rosy woke up, everything was different. . . .

Grandma was in the kitchen. She gave Rosy a big hug and told her that Dad had been sick during the night. Mom had taken him to the hospital. Grandma told Rosy not to worry — Dad would be home as soon as he was feeling better.

But Rosy did worry. The wind whistled around the house and rattled at the windows, and for the first Saturday ever, Rosy's dad wasn't there.

Rosy thought it might make her feel better to play with her dollhouse.

But when she opened it up, she gasped with surprise!
Something was different. . . .

It looked as if
a whirlwind had
blown through
the house!
Everything was
topsy-turvy —
even the dolls
looked surprised.

Then Rosy
saw some dusty
footprints going
upstairs to the
bedroom. And
tucked into
the little brass
bed was . . .

a fairy!

The fairy sat up, rubbing her eyes and yawning.

"Hello," she said. "I'm Thistle. I'm going to stay for a few nights, because I've hurt my wing. It's much nicer in here than sleeping in a flower in the garden. You don't mind, do you?"

Rosy was enchanted. She didn't mind at all. It was so exciting to have a real fairy in her dollhouse! Besides, she felt sorry for the fairy with her hurt wing.

Thistle's hair stuck out around her head like dandelion fluff. She was dressed in leaves and petals, and she had very muddy feet.

"I'm hungry," Thistle said, "but the food in this house is just pretend. What's for breakfast?"

Rosy ran outside and picked raspberries and rose petals
and all sorts of things to make a perfect fairy breakfast.

She also filled a dollhouse cup with rainwater and took everything back to Thistle. But it wasn't Thistle's idea of a perfect breakfast.

"Have you got any potato chips?" she asked.

Rosy couldn't help noticing that Thistle was very messy. She ate her chips with her mouth open and spilled her drink everywhere. But Rosy didn't mind. She just wanted to take care of the little fairy.

Rosy didn't tell anyone about Thistle. She kept her bedroom door closed, and Rosy and Thistle played together in secret. The fairy had made herself quite at home in Rosy's dollhouse.

At bath time, Thistle splashed around in the dollhouse bathtub like a sparrow in a puddle. Then Rosy rubbed some cream on Thistle's sore wing and put two tiny bandages on it to make it better.

That evening, Mom came
back from the hospital. She told
Rosy that Dad was feeling much
better and would be home soon.
And when Rosy settled down
to sleep, she could see a tiny
light glowing in the dollhouse,
and she didn't feel quite so
worried about Dad anymore.

As the days passed, Thistle began to feel better too. And as the fairy's wing got stronger, Rosy helped her to practice flying again.

Thistle wasn't like all the sweet little fairies in Rosy's storybooks. She was funny and noisy and full of mischief. She bounced on the bed and drew on the walls. She tried on all the dolls' clothes and moved the furniture into funny places. She spilled things and she dropped things and she scattered fairy dust everywhere.

But Rosy loved her.

Then, at last, one sunny afternoon,
the front door opened and Dad was
home! Rosy flung her arms around
him. She was so happy he was back!

They all sat down together and ate the special cake that Rosy and Grandma had made.

Afterward, Rosy cuddled up to Dad.

"Just me and my Rosy Posy," he said with a smile. "Have you been busy with the dollhouse while I've been away?"

Rosy whispered in his ear and told him all about Thistle and how she had been helping to make her better. She also told him about how messy and mischievous Thistle was.

Dad listened very carefully.

"Do you think I could meet her too?" he asked.

Together, they went up to Rosy's room and looked in the dollhouse. Every room was a mess, but Thistle was nowhere to be seen.

"She was here. She was!" cried Rosy.

Dad gave her a big hug.

"I can see she was!" He laughed. "You must have done such a good job of looking after Thistle that now her wing is better and she has flown back home."

Together, Rosy and Dad picked up all the furniture, tidied the pretend food, and carefully put the tiny cups and plates back on the table. They cleaned the scribbles off the walls and blew away the last of the fairy dust.

But Dad left out a tiny piece of cake for Thistle,
just in case. . . .